CLICK, CLACK, Quackity-Quack

An Alphabetical Adventure

by doreen cronin
and
betsy lewin

SCHOLASTIC INC.
New York Toronto London Auckland Sydney
Mexico City New Delhi Hong Kong Buenos Aires

a

Animals awake

b

beneath blue blankets.

Clickety-clack!

Duck dashing,

d

e

eggs emptying.

Flippity-flip!

Goats
grooming,

hens
helping,

i inchworms inching.

j Jumpity-jump!

Kittens kicking,

leaping,

licking.

Mice munching,

nibbling nibbles.

Only one pig peeking.

Rain raining,

sheep sleeping.

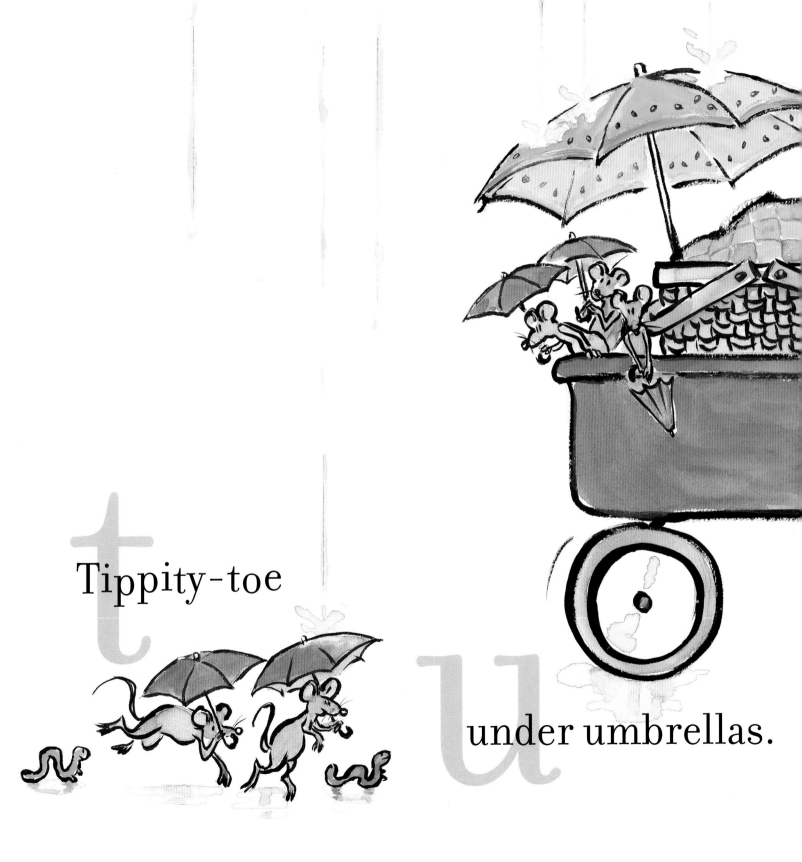

Tippity-toe

under umbrellas.

Vroom!

W

Watermelons
waiting.

marks the picnic spot.

Yawns yawning!

Z z z z zz

ZZ Z Z Z Z Z Z Z Z Z Z.

For my bunnies

—D. C.

To Julia. Welcome to the world.

—B. L.

No part of this publication may be reproduced, stored in a retrieval system, or transmitted in any form or by any means, electronic, mechanical, photocopying, recording, or otherwise, without written permission of the publisher. For information regarding permission, write to Atheneum Books for Young Readers, Simon & Schuster Children's Publishing Division, 1230 Avenue of the Americas, New York, NY 10020.

ISBN-13: 978-0-439-89975-8

ISBN-10: 0-439-89975-3

Text copyright © 2005 by Doreen Cronin.
Illustrations copyright © 2005 by Betsy Lewin. All rights reserved.
Published by Scholastic Inc., 557 Broadway, New York, NY 10012, by arrangement with Atheneum Books for Young Readers, Simon & Schuster Children's Publishing Division. SCHOLASTIC and associated logos are trademarks and/or registered trademarks of Scholastic Inc.

12 11 10 9 8 7 6 5 4 3 2 1   6 7 8 9 10 11/0

Manufactured in China   46

First Scholastic printing, September 2006

Book design by Ann Bobco

The text for this book is set in Filosofia.

The illustrations for this book are rendered in brush and watercolor.